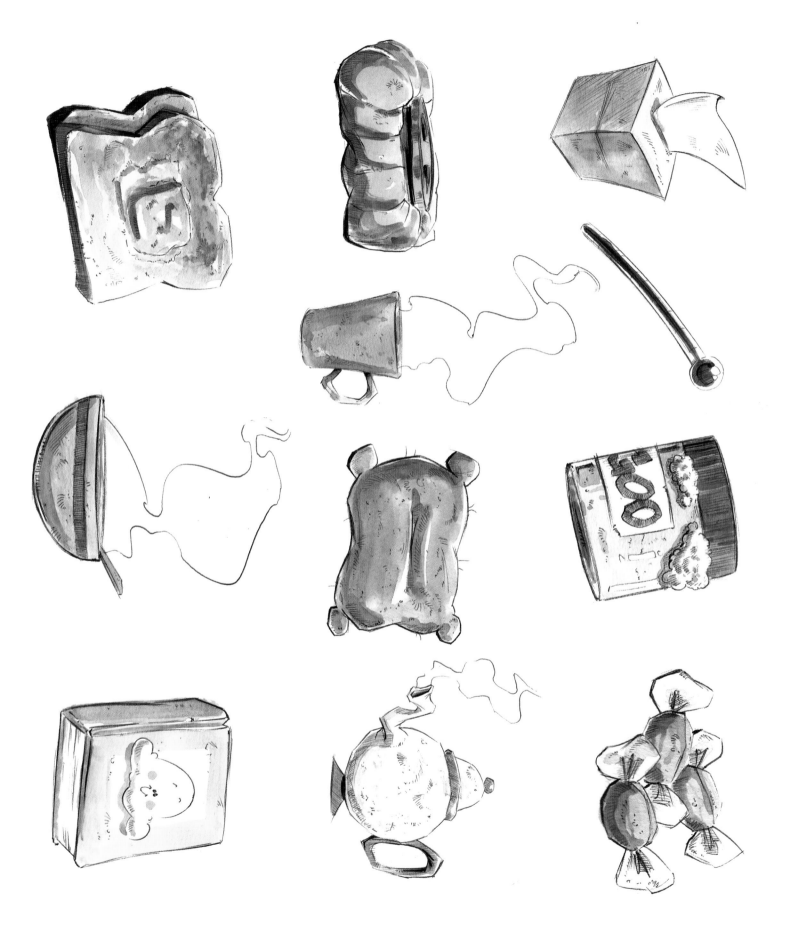

Mulberry Street Publishing
Orange County, CA. www.mulberrystreetpublishing.com

Library of Congress Control Number: 2019908025

Michaels, Andie

Achoo! Achoo! I've Got the Flu / by Andie Michaels ; illustrations by Mark Hernandez

Summary: Sad and alone on his birthday, Lion is super excited when his friends show up to throw him a surprise party. But the day takes another unexpected turn when his four friends come down with the flu one at a time, leaving the lion to care for his sick and demanding friends.

ISBN 978-1-7330663-0-3

[1.Sick-Fiction. 2.Lions-Fiction. 3.Bears-Fiction. 4.Stories that rhyme. 5.Friendships-Fiction. 6.Humorous. 7.Birthdays-Fiction.]

First Edition: August, 2019
10 9 8 7 6 5 4 3 2 1

Andie Michaels www.andiemichaels.com

Printed and bound in the United States.

Achoo! Achoo! Achoo!

I've Got the Flu

Written by Andie Michaels

Illustrated by Mark Hernandez

Mulberry Street Publishing, Orange County, CA. www.mulberrystreetpublishing.com

Chick-a-dee-dee, the blue bird sang.

The lion slumped, his four paws hang.

When *knock-knock-knock*, BANG, the doorbell rang,

he peeked outside to view.

They shout, "Surprise!"
tears filled his eyes,
his stomach full of
butterflies.
The lion cries,
he slapped his thighs,
"Balloons and flowers too!!"

While Lion filled the floral vase,
Gorilla tied balloons in place.
Then hippo sneezed in Lion's face.
Gorilla snorted, "Ewwww!"

The polar bear baked birthday cakes.
Gorilla guzzled gobs of shakes.
The hippo wheezed, "My tummy-aches,"
then sniffed and sneezed,

Achoo!

The milkshakes peppered Polar Bear.
The cakes clung on Gorilla's hair.
The lion's food flung everywhere
and Rhino's food flung too.

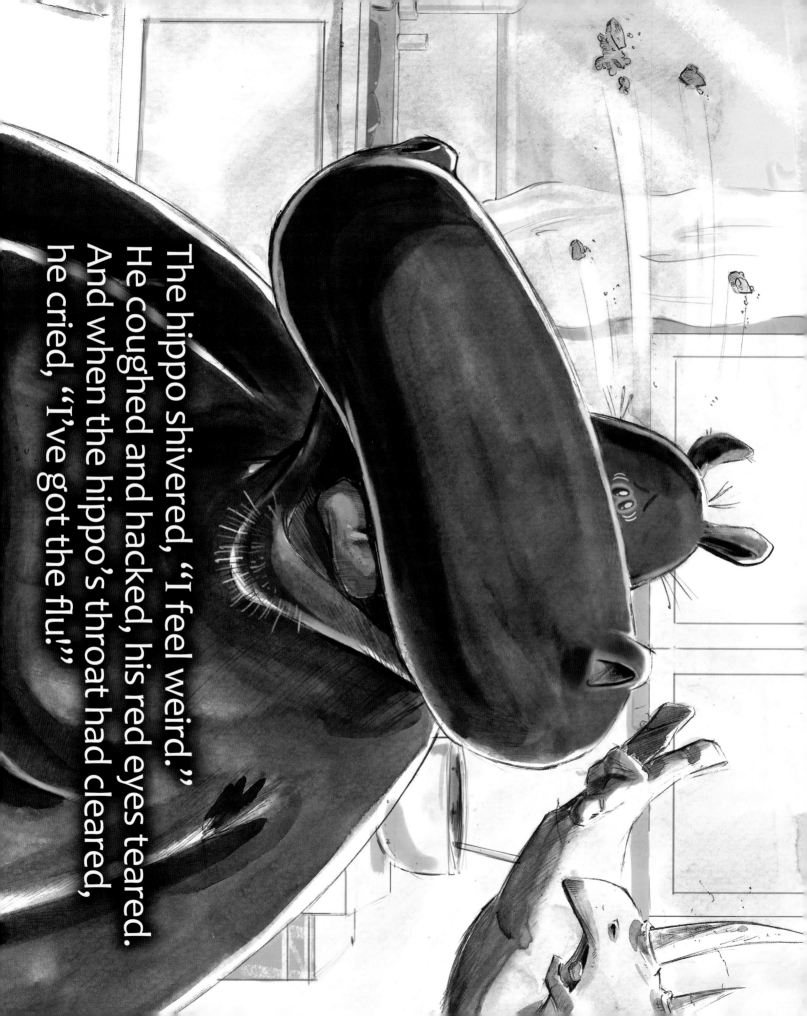

The hippo shivered, "I feel weird."
He coughed and hacked, his red eyes teared.
And when the hippo's throat had cleared,
he cried, "I've got the flu!"

The polar bear and Lion stared
as Hippo's runny nostrils flared.
Gorilla wrapped him up and blared,
"His cheeks are hot! It's true!"

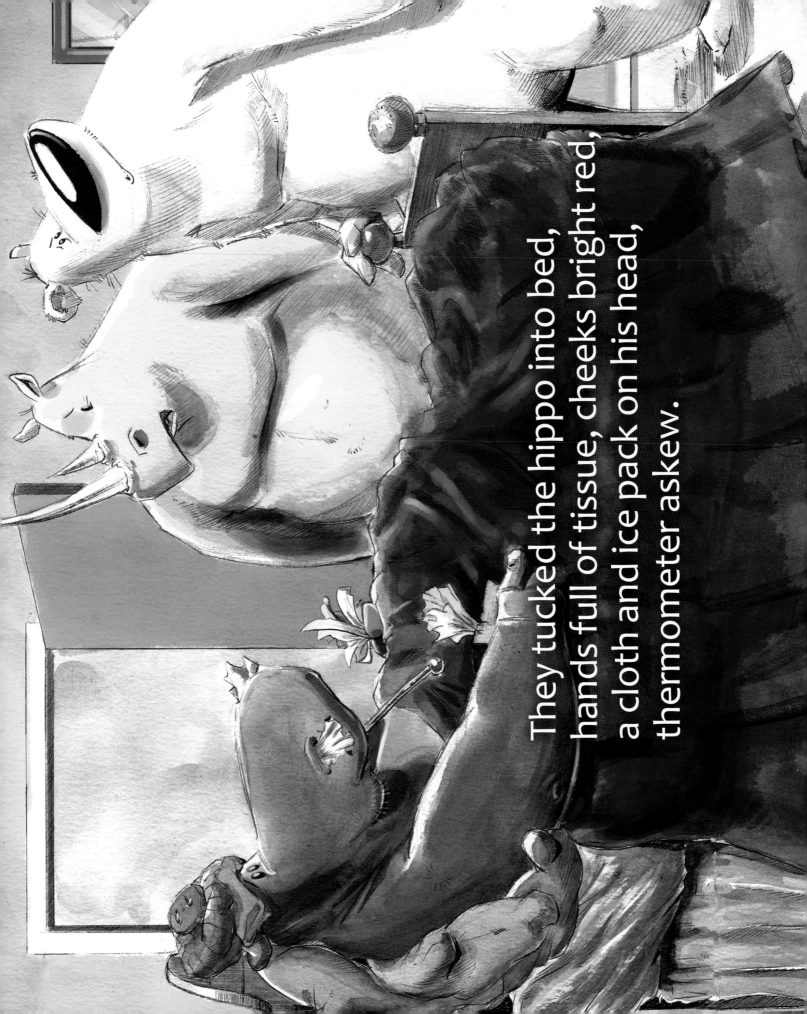

They tucked the hippo into bed,
hands full of tissue, cheeks bright red,
a cloth and ice pack on his head,
thermometer askew.

Gorilla sniffled, "I feel weird."
He coughed and hacked, his red eyes teared.
And when Gorilla's throat had cleared,
he cried, "I've got it too!"

The rhino said, "Scooch in to bed."
Gorilla asked for toasted bread.
They covered him, they cooled his head,
then smeared his chest with goo.

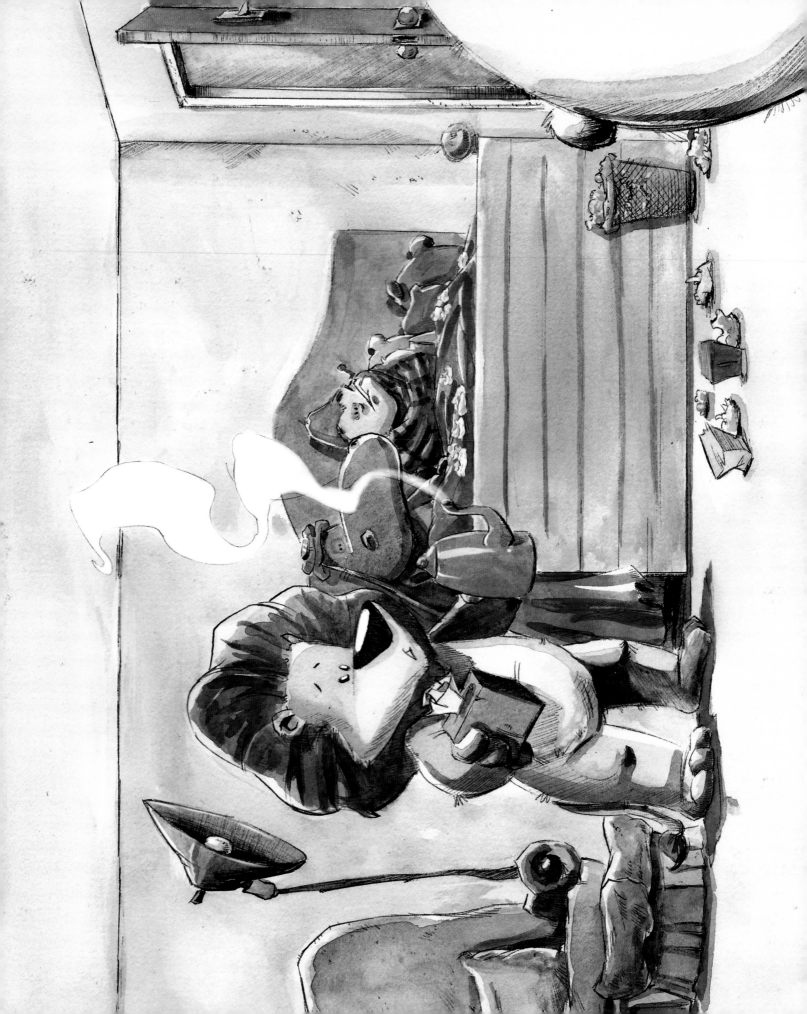

Gorilla burbled, "Herbal tea."
The hippo snorted, "Sugar free."
The rhino pleaded, "Make it three."
They sniffed, they wiped, they blew.

The hippo hankered soup and bread.
Gorilla wanted his spoon-fed.
The rhino whimpered, "Rub my head.
We need more blankets too."

The polar bear shook, "I need more!"
He tugged, they yanked; the blanket tore.
First cold, then hot, their bodies sore,
they wheezed then sneezed,

Achoo!

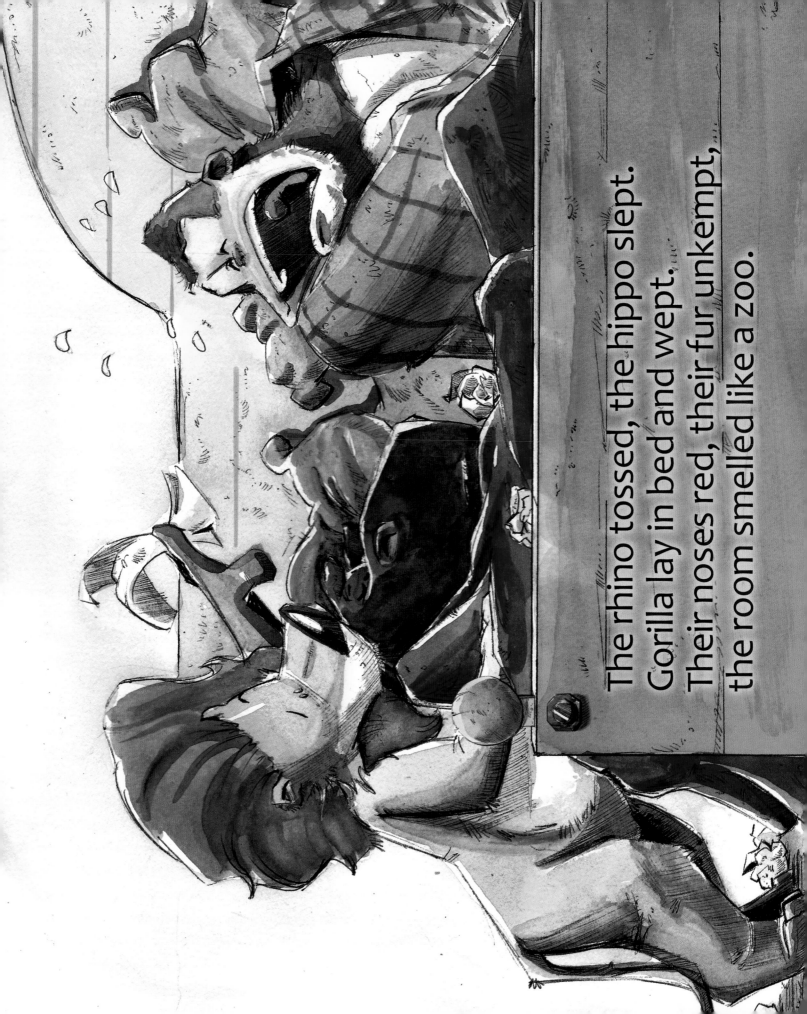

The rhino tossed, the hippo slept.
Gorilla lay in bed and wept.
Their noses red, their fur unkempt,
the room smelled like a zoo.

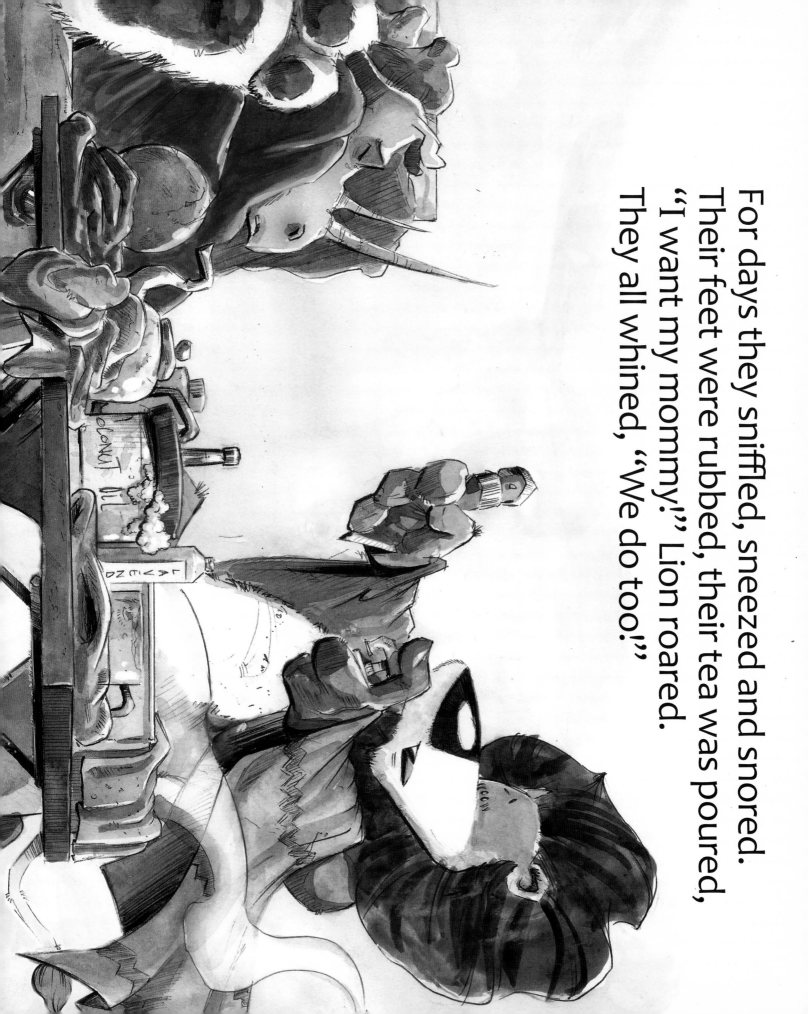

For days they sniffled, sneezed and snored.
Their feet were rubbed, their tea was poured,
"I want my mommy!" Lion roared.
They all whined, "We do too!"

Then on the day they all were well they rode their bike, they rang the bell. Fresh air at last! They all could smell. Birds sang. The sky was blue.

Then Lion shivered, "I feel weird."
He coughed and hacked, his red eyes teared.
And when the lion's throat had cleared,
he cried, "I'VE GOT THE FLU!"

They rushed the lion into bed,
hands full of tissue, cheeks bright red,
a cloth and ice pack on his head,
thermometer askew.

For days he sniffled, sneezed and snored.
His feet were rubbed, his tea was poured,
"Please rub my tummy,"
"And read a story too." Lion roared.

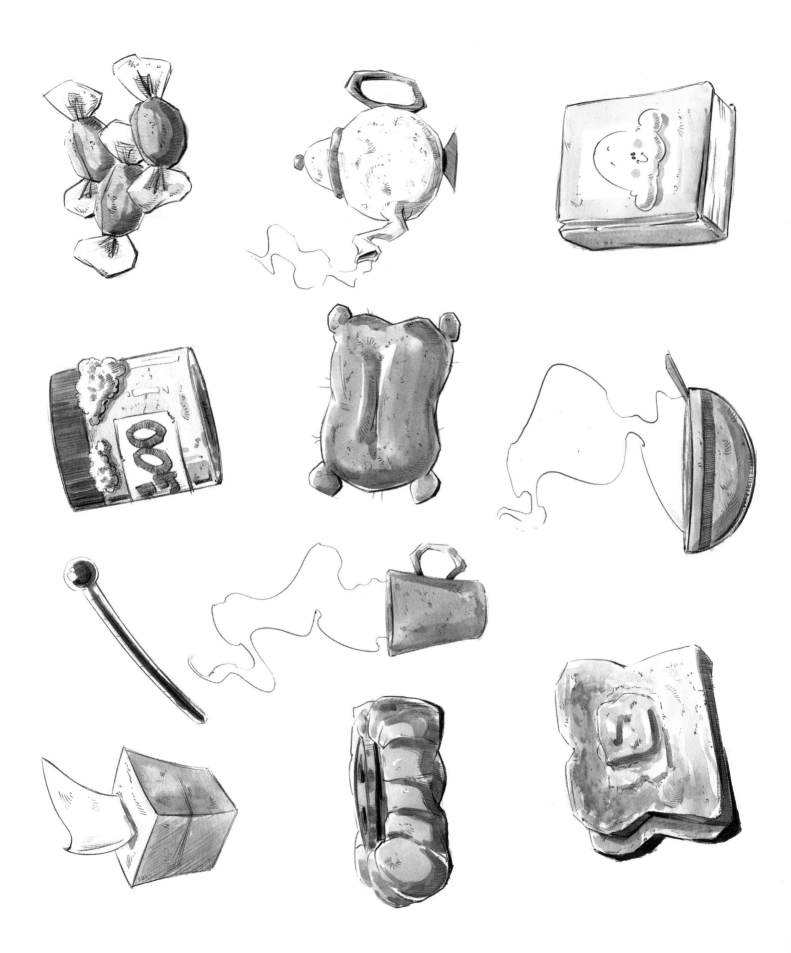